The Story of
Mrs. Santa Claus

Written by Bethanie Tucker
Illustrated by Crystal McLaughlin

Waterway Publishers
www.waterwaypublishers.com

Long, long ago,
before she was married to Santa Claus,
Mrs. Santa was a little girl.
She lived near the North Pole in
a house made of ice.

Many animals lived close to her house, and she knew how to talk to them. "You can talk to us so well that we will call you Fauna," the animals told her. "The name Fauna means animal."

Fauna and the animals liked to play games.
Fauna's favorite game was to ride on the
backs of the flying reindeer
to see animals who lived
in faraway places.

One morning when they returned from
their ride, Fauna was sad.
"The baby animals in other countries
don't have any toys to play with,"
she said.

The littlest reindeer thought for a moment, then said, "You can make toys for them." The other reindeer clapped their hooves together. "That's a great idea!" they cheered. "You make the toys, and we will help you take them to the baby animals."

Fauna put her hand to her chin and rubbed it, then answered, "We can try, but we don't have much time. We need to give the animals their toys before the end of the year, while they are still babies."

Fauna got busy right away.
She made rubber balls for the seals
and balls of yarn for the kittens.
Soon she was making swings
for the monkeys.

Fauna worked as fast as she could, but the days and weeks flew by. Before long, it was December—the last month of the year—and Fauna had not finished making the toys. She didn't know what to do, so she decided to take a long walk so she could think.

Fauna walked and walked ... and pretty soon
she had walked all the way to
the North Pole.
Fauna was very tired, so she sat down,
leaned against the pole, and went to sleep.

Fauna slept for a long time.
When she woke up, she heard a strange
noise behind her. Very quietly she stood up
and peeked around the pole.

Fauna could not believe what she saw.

There, on the other side of the North Pole, was a boy. He was dressed in a red velvet suit and black boots, and he was sitting on the snow, crying.

Suddenly the boy saw Fauna. He stopped crying and wiped his eyes.

"Who are you?" he asked.

"My name is Fauna," she replied.
"Who are you?"
"My name is Santa," the boy said
as he stood up and shook Fauna's hand.

"Why were you crying?" Fauna asked.

"I have made toys for all the good boys and girls all over the world," Santa said.

Fauna was surprised. She wondered why making toys would make anyone sad, but instead she asked,
"How did you make so many toys?"

"Elves helped me," Santa answered.

"Elves? You have elves for helpers?" Fauna exclaimed. "Then why are you sad?"

 "I'm sad because I don't have a way to *take* the toys to all the girls and boys," Santa answered.
"I can't *walk* all the way around the world."

Fauna got quiet for a moment, then she smiled a big smile. "Flying reindeer could help you," she said.
"Flying reindeer?" Santa repeated, a puzzled look on his face. "I've never seen a reindeer that can *fly* ..."

"I have lots of friends who are flying
reindeer," Fauna explained.
"And I'm sure they would be happy to take
you and your toys around
the world in a sleigh."

"I have gone with them," she added.
"I know they can make the trip in one night."

Santa was so excited that he jumped up and down. "Flying reindeer can help me take my toys!" he shouted. Suddenly Santa stopped jumping and looked at Fauna. "Why do *you* look so sad?" Santa asked.

"I am sad because
I wanted to make toys for all the
baby animals in the world,"
Fauna said.
"But I don't have time to finish them
before the end of the year, while the
animals are still babies."

"Now I have an idea for *you!*" Santa said. His eyes were twinkling. "The elves can help you finish making your toys."
"The elves? Do you really think they *would?*" Fauna asked. "Of course they would," Santa replied. "The elves are wonderful helpers."

Fauna and Santa were so happy
they joined hands and danced in a circle.
Finally Fauna stopped dancing.
"I need to go and get everything ready
for the elves," she said. So she
waved goodbye and ran home.

The next morning 100 elves came to Fauna's house.
They worked day and night, and on December 24th, one week before the end of the year, they finished making the toys.

That night Fauna and Santa met at
the North Pole because that is where they
had first learned to know each other.
Fauna's sleigh was loaded with animal toys,
and Santa's sleigh was filled with
toys for boys and girls.

All night long
Fauna and her reindeer took toys
to animals,
and Santa and his reindeer
took toys to girls and boys.

The next morning Santa and Fauna returned
to the North Pole at exactly the same time.
They jumped out of their sleighs and,
once again, joined hands.
The elves gathered 'round.

"Thank you for your help,"
Fauna said to
Santa and the elves.

"Thank *you* for telling me about flying reindeer," Santa said to Fauna. Then he went to both sleighs and gave each reindeer a hug.

"Teamwork is great!"
shouted everyone with a big cheer. From that time on, Fauna, Santa, the elves, and the reindeer worked together. Year after year they made toys and took them to baby animals and good boys and girls all over the world.

When Fauna and Santa got older,
they fell in love and got married.
Mr. and Mrs. Santa Claus built their
house at the very same place they
had first met—the North Pole.

And to this very day
Fauna and Santa still make
toys for the good boys and girls
and for the baby animals
all around the world.

At Christmas time you can see
their presents—and, if you look very,
very closely, you might even be able to see
Fauna and Santa late at night on
Christmas Eve.

The Story of Mrs. Santa Claus
Written by Bethanie H. Tucker
Illustrated by Crystal McLaughlin
ISBN 10: 0-976239-00-0
ISBN 13: 978-0-976239-00-0

Project credits

Copy editing and proofing	Dan Shenk
Cover layout	Frieda Probst
Book layout	Paula Nicolella

Other books by Bethanie H. Tucker (for more information, visit www.ahaprocess.com):

Tucker Signing Strategies for Reading

Mr. Base Ten Invents Mathematics

The Journey of Al and Gebra to the Land of Algebra

Reading by Age 5

Visit www.mrssantaclausbooks.com to learn more about *The Story of Mrs. Santa Claus* books.